UNWRAPPING THE PACK

OMEGAVERSE HOLIDAY QUICKIES

CLOVER HOLLOWAY

Book Cover: Unfortunate Designs

Independently Published by Unfortunate Productions LLC

Print ISBN: 979-8-9913742-6-2

BLURB

Mollie's pack has a fun Christmas surprise for her. When Mollie comes home and finds the house quiet, she follows the clues left for her to find her pack waiting for her in their bedroom with...things in boxes that probably shouldn't be in boxes. After a show that has Mollie laughing so hard she's in tears, the mood gets quite a bit sexier. It's definitely a white Christmas this year, even if there isn't any snow.

Omegaverse Holiday Quickies are novelettes with more smut than plot. They are meant to be a fun escape with no angst that you can read in one sitting. Have fun and get your spice on!

Just remember y'all, the tinsel makes it festive.

AUTHOR'S NOTE

A note about the Omegaverse Holiday Quickies series. We all love Omegaverse books with lots of character development and conflict resolution, and of course heats, but sometimes you just want a short little palate cleanser to read in between longer novels, or while you're in the waiting room at the doctor's office, or the school pick up line...you catch my drift.

That's where the Omegaverse Holiday Quickies series comes in! I love reading those short instalove/instalust where a OTT man falls hard and fast for a damsel he rescued from the woods/mountain/mafia/ex/etc, but I usually only find them in the contemporary genres. I wanted to capture that same vibe but with an Omegaverse twist.

All of these stories will be of existing packs, or insta-love pack formation, with no angst or third act breakups. They are very short, and meant to be fast, fun, and totally smutty.

They are also light on the Omegaverse pitfalls, and won't always center around a heat. The spice will be spicin' though, I promise you that! If you aren't familiar with Omegaverse, take a look at the short primer I included next.

All my books are queer. The worlds they are set in are queer-normative and there will always be a wide mix of relationship pairings, dynamics, and genders. Even if the primary relationship is a man and a woman, all my characters are pan unless otherwise stated. If that's not something you're comfortable with, my books likely aren't for you.

There are also explicit adult scenes mixed with a healthy dose of kink. Please read the content considerations before diving in.

I really hope you love this series, because I have so many ideas for more holiday quickies!

Stay lucky,
Clover 🍀

WHAT IS OMEGAVERSE?

Omegaverse is a subgenre that takes place in an alternate universe loosely based on canid culture. Similar to wolf shifters, they form packs and have a hierarchy, but there are no shifters in my Omegaverse. There are different *designations* of people - most commonly alpha, beta, and omega. Each Omegaverse may have different designations, rules, and lore depending on the author. In this primer the rules will be specific to the universe I created for these characters, and some details may not be the same as you've read before.

Some things most every Omegaverse has in common though are designations (A/B/O), heats, scents, and knots.

Alphas

Alphas are usually the strongest and most dominant members of society. They are usually big and muscular, and some may have more *alpha power* than others. They can *bark* other designations into submission, forcing them to follow their commands. They also have a special feature at the base of their penises called a *knot*. The knot will swell when the alpha orgasms, and if they are having penetrative sex then it will *lock* them inside their partner. Alphas can be driven into a *rut* when overly aroused.

Alphas are often in positions of power and will behave based on their alpha instincts. Their scents are strong and they will bite a partner to *bond* them.

Betas

Betas are what most people would consider a "regular" person. They are the most common designation in society and aren't as affected by hormones and pheromones. They do not have knots and won't go into a rut.

There are some worlds where betas may be considered less valuable because they are essentially normal humans. In this world, betas are known to be excellent additions to packs because they are level-headed and can balance out the extremes of alphas and omegas.

Omegas

Omegas are usually the rarest and most valued designation in society. Because of their low numbers, one omega may form a pack with several alphas and betas. Omegas are generally submissive and natural caretakers. Omegas have heats where their bodies drive them to breed. They will have insatiable sexual appetites and they may need several partners to satisfy them. If omegas are not knotted during their heat, it can be extremely painful and sometimes dangerous for the omega.

In some worlds, omegas may be considered the lowest rung of society, and even like property. They could be barred from getting jobs or may be otherwise controlled by their families or their alphas. They can be any gender and sometimes assigned male at birth (AMAB) people can get pregnant.

Heats and Ruts

This is a state where omegas and alphas are completely driven by their hormones to copulate. The heat could be on a regular schedule much like a woman's period, or they could be unpredictable. Both options are common tropes in the genre. When in a heat or rut, omegas will often beg for a *bonding bite*, and alphas are driven to *bite* and *claim* their omegas.

These episodes may be controlled by *heat suppressants* or *rut blockers*.

Scent Matches

Scent is super important in Omegaverse. Everyone has some type of scent, everything from sandalwood to strawberry shortcake and more. Alphas and omegas will have the strongest scents, and betas will have milder scents. When someone finds someone with a scent that is utterly irresistible, they are *scent matches*. This is akin to fated mates. Some universes will have different levels of scent matches (scent sympathetic, scent match, soul scent, etc).

Often if there is an incompatible alpha or omega, then they will smell terrible to the main characters. Usually their scents can indicate mood, souring or burning when they are upset, or sweeter when they are aroused. Mates will often *scent mark* each other by rubbing their *scent glands* or cheeks along the other's skin to *claim* each other.

Mates/Bonding

As you read above, scent matches often indicate mates. When an alpha claims a beta or omega, they will bite them to mark them with a *bonding bite*. The bonds will work differently in each universe, but most commonly bonded mates will have a two way mental connection where they can sense each other's moods. Sometimes alphas will force bonds on people who are not their willing mates, and sometimes you have to accept the connection for a bond to stick. Sometimes only the alphas need to make the bite, but sometimes both partners need to claim each other to complete the bond. This is probably the most varied tenet in Omegaverse and it doesn't mean any one is incorrect.

CONTENT CONSIDERATIONS

This is an adult story with explicit sexual content. It's more smut than plot. Like, way more. The characters in this story are polyamorous and have different relationships with each other. They are also an established pack, so there will not be a heat or ruts, and they are already bonded.

In addition to bad dancing, you will find fingering, penetrative sex, anal sex, cunnilingus, fellatio, double penetration, face fucking, light degradation, light bondage (wrists tied), rough sex, unprotected sex, questionable use of tinsel, and hand necklaces.

"Hellooo!" My voice echoed off the tall ceilings of our foyer. Any second now Finn would come bounding down the stairs like an excited golden retriever, complete with the requisite body tackle and slobber. It's one of my favorite things about my shaggy haired alpha, he's always excited to see me. Three years of living together and that enthusiasm hasn't waned.

Turning to shut the door, I lock the deadbolt and toss my keys in the bowl on the console table where they land with a soft clink. No one has greeted me by the time I shuck my coat, hang it on the rack, and dust the fluffy snowflakes from my hair. Which is...odd.

In fact, the house is eerily quiet for six pm on a Friday. Finn works from home, and Holden ends his work week by leaving early, usually around three o'clock. The only one I wouldn't expect to be here is Elijah. My hunky beta usually hits the gym before he comes home, and I can't say I hate it. When he walks in the door all sweaty, his sweet citrus scent blooming from his workout—yeah. That makes Mollie a very happy omega.

Also a horny one. Tomato tomahto.

I take two steps forward before calling out again. "Finn? Holden?" No answer. "Eli? Is anybody home?"

I'm about to pull out my phone when a glint catches my eye, drawing my gaze to the carpet runner beneath my feet. Is that...tinsel?

I bend over to grab a handful, and sure enough, it's silvery tinsel. And it's spread all the way down the hallway. After some consideration, I decide it looks like a trail.

This has Finn written all over it. Smiling, I follow the line of silver strands down the corridor, where it then turns left to go up the stairs. At the first landing, I find a ribbon has replaced the tinsel trail and I burst out laughing.

I'd bet good money that he wanted to string the ribbon from wherever he is (or whatever he has waiting for me) to the front door, but he ran out and had to improvise. Good thing we don't have any pets or we'd be dealing with their sparkle shits for days.

Clearing my head of that disgusting thought, I pick up the ribbon and slowly thread it through my hands as I walk. At the top of the stairs, the path leads me to the right, toward the pack bedroom and my nest. The door to the bedroom is shut, and the ribbon runs underneath it, disappearing into the darkness beyond the gap.

Something tickles my eardrums, so I pause, then tilt my head to listen harder. Bells? No, wait, it's music.

The upbeat melody of Sleigh Ride gets louder the closer I get to the door. When the song ends, I hear soft snickers and an oomph, and I can imagine my guys bickering softly. Maybe even Finn elbowing Holden to stay quiet. Before I can eavesdrop more, though, White Christmas plays, effectively nixing any chance I had at listening in.

I won't torture them by waiting out here, that's just cruel. Plus, I really want to see what they're up to. Typical omega here, I love surprises. A huge grin is on my face as I burst into the room, then come to a dead stop.

I'm going to kill Finn. Earlier today he sent a message to our secret group chat—the one we have so we can shop for our omega for Christmas—saying he had 'the best idea ever,' which is always concerning.

I love Finn like a brother. Well, a brother I get naked and have group sex with. It's probably best not to continue down that line of thought. The point is, he's pack and he means well, but sometimes his ideas are wild at best and batshit crazy at worst.

Like the time he rented a full size dunk tank, like the ones you'd see at a carnival, for Mollie's thirtieth birthday bash. It wasn't even like the party was themed where a dunk tank would be appropriate. Finn tends to get an idea in his head and run with it, not always thinking about logistics or consequences. Needless to say, it ended with all of us soaking wet, hurting from falling against the metal sides of the tank over and over again, and bruised egos. It did make our omega smile, though.

Then there was this time he brought home ducklings from the farm supply store. He said they were on sale. How *ducks* go on sale is beyond me, but suddenly we were frantically googling what ducklings eat and how to build an enclosure. His *sale ducks* went from a good deal to costing us hundreds of dollars. Ducks are also messy as fuck. When they became full sized monsters, we had to rehome them because they just kept reproducing. Mollie did love cuddling the little creatures though.

Which is why I even went along with this asinine idea of my pack mate's this time. I'd suffer any of Finn's schemes to make our omega smile.

"Fuck, why is this so itchy?" I whine. "And the box is slipping. This cannot be safe for our junk."

The sweet holiday music playing is completely incongruous to the scene of three large men nearly naked and sparkling under the Christmas lights. Finn shoots me a glare at the same time Eli whacks my chest with the back of my hand.

"Shhh! She should be home soon!" Finn whisper hisses.

Like he summoned her, the door opens to reveal our stunning—albeit confused—omega.

A m I really seeing what I think I'm seeing? The room
is dark, only the faint multi-color glow of Christmas
lights giving any visibility. A Bluetooth speaker is on the
dresser, The dulcet tones of Bing Crosby completely incon-
gruent to the main attraction in front of me.

Finn, Holden, and Eli are standing shoulder to shoulder
at the foot of the bed. Completely naked.

Well, that's not entirely true. They each have a Santa
hat on, the Pom Pom flopped adorably to the side. Draped
over their shoulders like a festive feather boa, are shiny
tinsel garlands. Finn's is silver, Holden's red, and poor Eli
rounds out the group with green. His expression is tight,
and I know he's only going along with this to make me
happy. God, I love him so much.

I love all of them so much it hurts.

As my hungry gaze drags down their bare torsos, the
Christmas lights create shadows that highlight their cut
figures. Call me Dora because I'd like to explore all those
dips and valleys.

Preferably with my tongue.

What's just below those obliques, however, has me throwing my head back and laughing. I'm talking loud and boisterous with a side of unladylike snorting.

In front of "the goods," they each hold a wrapped present. When I finally can form real human words again, I ask, "What? Are you...you don't...are your—"

"Oh! Wait! The song!" I'm cut off abruptly by Finn shouting. "We have to play the song!" He lifts the lid to his box and pulls out his phone, tapping away at the screen.

Holden looks at him incredulously. "Was your phone seriously in the box with your—"

"SHHH!" Finn hisses, then the song switches. The Christmas classic that was playing gives way to something far more unhinged.

My jaw drops. "You didn't."

The bass rises and my men all begin dancing sensually. Well, as sensually as they can. Elijah has the most rhythm, so he pulls off the sexy scene. Holden is doing body rolls, the lickable muscles on his stomach flexing on each pass. Finn... Oh my dear, sweet Finn. He's doing some sort of thrusting move with his hips, but he nearly loses his box and has to do some contortionist level maneuvering to avoid dropping it.

As hard as I try to hold it together, I lose it when the chorus kicks in and they start singing. I can barely hear the lyrics over my wheezing.

4

"It's my dick in a box
My knot in a box babe
It's my dick in a box
Ooh, my knot in a box girl"

This is embarrassing. It isn't even the concept of us wrapping our dicks up like we're in some early-2000's music video. It's the fact that two of the three of us have no rhythm. I think Finn may actually have negative rhythm.

Holden is rolling his body like he's the lead dancer in a male revue, dragging his hands over his body and shaking his ass. Occasionally he takes the end of his tinsel-garland-boa-thing and twirls it around like a burlesque tease. Compared to our third pack mate though, he may as well be a professional.

Finn is...I'm actually not entirely sure *what* Finn is doing. He started out shimmying his shoulders, which was weird but fine. Then was thrusting in the air like he was trying to knock out a champion boxer with just his penis.

He almost lost his box with that move. But now? Now he's attempting what I can only describe as some sort of sexy crab-walk. While twerking.

Mollie's eyes are as wide as saucers and her mouth is open in such shock that her jaw is at risk of hitting the floor. Color rises on her pretty cheeks as she takes us in and I'm unsure if it's embarrassment or arousal.

Taking our cue from The Disaster Formerly Known as Finn, we wiggle-dance our way forward until we're standing just a few steps from our omega. The song reaches its final crescendo and we all rip off the lids to our boxes, presenting our 'gifts' to our mate.

And she fucking loses it.

5

"Fuck, I cannot. I can't. You guys...I'm, I'm dying. Please. You actually...fucking...did it." It takes a while for me to get my words out between all the laughing and panting. Sure enough, in each of their boxes, is a dick. Their dicks. They cut a hole into the side that faces their body, and shoved their shafts through the makeshift glory hole.

The song ends, and I'm left staring at my bonded mates' cocks. All wrapped up for me like the perfect present. I smirk at Finn and reach into his box, dragging a red painted fingernail along the stop of his shaft. His hard-on twitches, and he looks at me with wide eyes. I lock my gaze with his, not looking away when I lick my palm then reach into the box again, this time wrapping my hand around his length and giving him a firm pump.

"Fuck! Mollie!" Finn yelps.

"What?" I smirk at him. "I thought these were my early Christmas presents. You had to know I'd want to play with my toys right away."

A strangled whine leaves his throat, his teeth digging

into his lower lip as he watches me work his cock while it's still in the box. His knot begins to swell, and he looks up at me with a mix of pleasure and panic on his face.

It's clear my sweet golden retriever alpha didn't think this all the way through, and if I make him come right now, his knot will swell and he'll be stuck with the box on his dick until he either cuts the cardboard off, or he deflates.

"Wait! Mollie, baby, wait. I don't wanna be stuck in this box!" Finn's voice gets higher pitched as he pleads with me. Holden and Elijah have smartly removed their boxes already and are stalking toward me.

Holden presses against my back and shoves his fingers into my hair, gripping it tight to yank my face to his. "Naughty omega. Your alpha is trying to give you a gift and you're torturing him." He crashes his lips to mine and licks into my mouth, his hold on my hair unrelenting. I whine when he pulls away, but his other hand slides up the front of my neck to lightly collar my throat. "Settle, omega." His deep baritone is laced with gravel, and slick drips down my thighs. The skirt I have on isn't going to absorb any of it. Hopefully one of my mates will clean it up with their tongue.

Eli grips my wrist that's in the box and tugs, forcing me to release Finn's cock. Finn gasps and frantically scrambles, managing to remove the prop before it's too late.

My beta maneuvers both hands behind my back, then uses the garland that was draped over his neck to bind them together. The tinsel is scratchy on my oversensitive skin, but he wraps the strand around several times before tying it off. He runs a finger between the binding and my skin to make sure it isn't too tight. We love to play with ropes and other toys, but we always make sure we're doing it safely.

Finished, Eli steps spins me into Holden's arms, my

back pressed to my alpha's chest, and steps aside, stroking his cock while he watches. Finn, now free of his cardboard confines, steps up to my front and reaches for me. He shoves my shirt up, rips the cups of my bra down, and flicks my newly exposed nipples.

"Ahh! Fuck!"

6

Finn

M ollie yelps and I smirk at her. "You deserve more than that for trying to mess with your gift, omega." I don't say more, choosing instead to lean forward and suck half her gorgeous tit into my mouth. I go to town, sucking and licking her tight nipple, roughly kneading her other breast until she moans. Holden still has his pretty hand necklace wrapped around Mollie's throat, so I take my time switching back and forth, making sure they each get the same rough treatment.

I'm an equal opportunity titty worshiper after all.

Mollie's breathing gets faster, and I glance up to see Holden licking and nipping along her skin from his bond mark to her earlobe. He's murmuring something sexy in her ear, and she's loving it. Holden has the filthiest mouth I've ever experienced. We aren't intimate with each other since Holden doesn't swing that way, but sometimes his words have me wanting to drop to my knees and present for him like a very good boy. I usually have to goad Eli into taking me rough and hard at that point.

"Did you like our gifts, omega?" Holden rumbles. "You

didn't seem to appreciate them, much. I didn't even hear a thank you. You're cruisin' for a bruisin', you little brat." A loud smack rings out. Mollie shrieks, then moans when Holden rubs the red mark he just put on her ass to soothe it.

"I get your cocks all the time. Doesn't seem all that special to me." Mollie taunts. Ohhhh she is aiming for some punishment, that's for sure. What started as a silly little surprise is about to turn into a showdown. One where we all win.

Eli steps up to my side, running a hand down my spine as he pushes me sideways a little to make room. He unexpectedly grips my hair and yanks me off the breast I was sucking. I don't have time to protest because he crashes his lips to mine and devours me.

"Oh shit. Yes." Mollie moans as she watches us, her sweet cotton candy scent blooming.

I push my body into his and grind my hips, our hard cocks rubbing one another. Needing more, I snake my hand between us to grab his cock. Precum drips from the swollen head, slicking my path up and down his shaft. He thrusts lightly into my hold, but doesn't stay connected long. He pulls away and licks a line up my face before turning to our writhing, whimpering omega.

Eli snares Mollie in a hard kiss, then peppers kisses down her body as he drops to his knees.

7

I'm moaning and panting and writhing, trying unsuccessfully to get the friction I need to come. Eli tears off my thong and pulls my right leg over his shoulder, using his thumbs to part my lower lips so he can have direct access to my clit. He doesn't lick it right away. Instead he blows a stream of cool air on the heated flesh, making my pussy clench. Just when I think he's going to warm it back up with his tongue, two thick fingers spear into me. I nearly come right then.

My beta is both the worst and best tease. He never follows the same routine, opting to change up his game plan every time. When I think he may eat me out, he'll flip the script and finger me instead. I'll beg him to fuck me, but he'll push my tits together to fuck them until I'm begging to swallow his cum. He makes sure we never get complacent in the bedroom, and I love everything he does to me.

The sweet build of an impending climax spreads through my body as my men work me over. Just when I am seeking that precipice, Eli pulls his fingers from my core. I nearly sob from the denied orgasm and immediate sense of emptiness that hits me. I should've known he wouldn't torture me for long, and I'm sure I'd have realized that if my brain wasn't hazed out of this solar system.

Strong hands grip my waist, pull me down to the floor, then yank me forward until I'm straddling Elijah's hips. I didn't even realize he'd laid down. I sit up on my knees to give him room, and he swipes the head of his cock through my folds a few times, coating it in my slick. It isn't long until he notches himself at my entrance and I sink down onto his thick shaft. I take him to the hilt in one go, and we both groan.

"Fuck," Eli grunts, "Moll, you're so goddamned wet." His fingertips dig into the flesh of my hips as he guides me to ride him. Not that I need much encouragement. I rock over him and fall forward to steal the grunts of pleasure straight from his lips. His lust flares in our bond, stoking the flames of my need even higher.

A hand grips my hair and uses the hold to pull me upright, the position sinking me down even further on Eli's cock. Lips feather over my nape and the mint chocolate scent that floods my senses tells me it's Holden before he even speaks.

"Can I have this sweet little ass, omega?" he growls into my skin, and I whine. With my hands still bound behind my back and his hold on my hair, I'm helpless and unable to move as Eli starts thrusting up into my pussy, each slam nearly hitting my cervix.

Another growl, this time followed by a wet finger trailing down my crack to rub over my tight back hole. "Words, omega." Holden's determined to kill me, I swear. "Do you want my cock in your tight ass? My knot? Yes or no?"

"Y-Yes!" I manage to cry and am rewarded with a harsh

kiss before I'm pressed forward to lie on Eli's chest again. I look up and see Finn roughly pleasuring himself, his eyes focused on our tangle of bodies.

"Alpha," I whine, but he shakes his head.

"Not yet, baby. Let Holden fill you up first, then I'll fuck your pretty throat." The filthy words from my sweetest alpha take me by surprise every time. Talk about a gentleman in the streets but a freak in the sheets.

Holden spreads my ass cheeks open and spits over my tight hole. He moves one hand down to follow the trail of saliva, using it to aid him pushing a finger in.

"Hold on, Elijah. Let me get our girl ready," Holden directs, and my beta sinks deep but stops thrusting. His hands are still locking my hips in place so I can't ride him like I so desperately want to. Holden swipes some of my slick from where Eli and I are connected, using it to work two, then three fingers into my ass, stretching me.

"Mmph...fuck, Holden. I can feel your fingers. Hurry up, I'm not sure how long I can hold out." Eli's voice is strained.

Suddenly I'm empty, but not for long. Holden replaces his finger with his slicked up cock and presses in slowly. I relish the burn, knowing it'll fade into pleasure soon. He pulls out and thrusts back in, sinking a little deeper each time until his hips are flush with my ass.

"Yes! Full. So full!" I cry, and my men start to move. They alternate their strokes, Eli pulling out as Holden pushes in. Then Holden is sliding out as Eli thrusts in. It doesn't take long until I'm a moaning, whimpering mess.

My alpha taking me from behind grasps my garland-wrapped wrists and pulls me upright, changing his angle entirely. "Your other mate is feeling neglected, omega."

Finn steps forward and guides his shaft to my mouth,

spreading his precum over my lips before tapping his cock head on them. I open eagerly, sticking out my tongue the way I know he likes.

"Good fucking girl," Finn growls, then gives me what I want. My tongue wraps around the underside of his cock as he pushes in until he hits the back of my throat. When I gag a little, he pulls back but I don't want him to. I try to chase after his retreating shaft and he chuckles darkly. "Don't worry, omega. You'll get my cum in your belly soon enough."

"Yes! Please, alpha! I need it!" I beg. He brings his cock toward my mouth again and pushes a hand into my hair.

"I'm gonna fuck your face omega. Can you feel Holden's hands?" he asks, and I nod. "Good. Hold onto his wrists, babygirl. Since you're tied up you won't be able to tap my thigh if you need a break, so if it gets to be too much you tap, squeeze, scratch—whatever you want—at Holden's wrists to get his attention, and he'll tell me. Okay?"

The thrusting in my pussy and ass has all but tapered off to a standstill during this exchange, and I know none of them will continue until I give clear, enthusiastic consent. It's one of things I love about these men. They make sure everyone is safe when we play, and it allows me to let go and allow them to use my body for pleasure. It's amazing.

"Yes, alpha." I tap Holden's wrist to assure them I'm clear on the rules.

8

"Open." Finn's one-word command causes more slick to coat Eli's cock and we all groan. I drop my jaw for my alpha, and he slides between my lips once more. As soon as he establishes a good rhythm, Holden and Eli start moving again, their movements uncoordinated at first until they get their timing down. This time they saw in and out of my body at the same time, both cocks filling me in concert, stretching me so fucking good.

My eyes water and my body shakes as my men utterly destroy me with pleasure. The first orgasm slams into me quickly, my mates fucking me through it without stopping. If anything, they get even more feral.

We're nothing but sweat-slick skin and desperate moans. Limbs tangled together and every one of my holes full. Love and lust pulse through our bonds until I don't know where mine starts and theirs begins. It's hot, and depraved, and perfect.

"I need you to come again before I knot you Mollie-girl," Holden grits out. "C'mon, omega. Milk our cocks so we can fill you up everywhere."

Elijah slides a hand between us and finds my clit, his fingers rubbing furious circles. Finn drops an arm and pinches my nipple, and I explode. Stars dance across my vision as I come, the pleasure so intense I rip my mouth off of Finn to tip back my head and scream.

"Fuck, fuck, I'm coming!" Eli groans as he slams deep and fills my pussy with his seed. Holden isn't far behind him. My alpha licks his bond mark on my neck as he forces his knot past the tight ring of muscle and lodges it in my ass. I come again as soon as we're locked together, Holden rutting into me as much as his knot will allow as he empties hot lashes of cum into my ass. So much that some tries to seep out around where we're joined.

"Tit's up, Omega," Finn heaves out between desperate gasps, and I whip my head up to look at him. His hand is flying so fast over his cock it's nearly a blur, his other hand fondling his balls. I push my chest out as much as I can with my hands still bound and my ass locked on a knot, then open my mouth and stick out my tongue, waiting for my alpha.

"Jesus fucking fuck, babygirl. You are so fucking hot," Finn praises. "That's right, take my cum." He moans long and loud as he paints my breasts in cum, some landing on my tongue. I greedily swallow it down, his cinnamon brandy flavor as addictive as a drug. Finn drops to his knees and kisses me gently, uncaring that he can taste himself on my lips. He pulls back, admiring his work of art and swipes two fingers through some of the cum on my chest. He leans around me, extending his hand until he can shove those same fingers into Eli's mouth. My beta sucks off every drop and all four of us groan at the sight.

Finn unbinds my wrists then helps maneuver Holden and me so we're laying on our sides, and Elijah slips out of my pussy with an obscene noise. He makes his way to the bathroom, and when I hear water running, I know my beta is getting a warm cloth to clean me up. Finn lays in front of me, peppering kisses all over my face and whispering words of praise. Holden rubs his large hands up and down my spine soothingly as we wait for his knot to come down.

Elijah comes back just as Holden slides out of me, leaving me deliciously sore. My sweet beta gently wipes over my chest and breasts, then down to my pussy and ass to clean up everyone's cum before it dries and gets gross. Combined with the love and pride they send me through the bond, the effect is so soothing I nearly fall asleep.

Strong arms slide under my knees and around my back, lifting with ease to cuddle me into a warm, bare chest. Decadent mint chocolate caresses my senses. Holden. He strides to the bed and Eli pulls back the covers. Holden slides us into the soft bedding, settling me in the crook of his arm, half draped over his chest as he purrs. Elijah crawls in to lie beside me, and Finn trips over one of the discarded boxes in his haste to join us. My golden retriever alpha doesn't want to be left out.

After a few minutes of shifting to get comfortable, peace settles over our pack. The bonds hum with contentment. I smile, knowing I can't help but to be a little bit of a brat yet again.

"So, how are you all gonna top this next year?"

My mates all laugh softly, and I thank fate again for bringing my pack together. There's no one else I'd rather be silly in love with. No where else I'd rather be than here, between them. Just before I fall asleep, I send up a Christmas wish that my pack will always be this in love for the rest of our days.

ABOUT THE AUTHOR

Clover Holloway is the cozier side of Unfortunate Reads, writing steamy monster and omegaverse romance that will make you swoon and sweat.

A long time romance reader turned author, she just can't help but make her stories cozy. She's an ADHD agent of chaos so her book topics may vary wildly, but you can always expect an HEA. She's an avid fan of traditional millennial customs including craft breweries, monstera plants, and skinny jeans.

Get lucky at cloverholloway.com.

ALSO BY CLOVER HOLLOWAY

Welcome to Bone Town

Adventure Omegaverse co-written with Thea Masen

Knot Letting Go

Olympic Omegaverse co-written with Thea Masen

Slip into Me

A short eel-shifter, fated mates novella.

Originally published in the Strange Love charity anthology.

Taking a Tumble

Meet cute with a dad-bod demon pet shop owner and a curvy, confident human woman.

Part of the Ghostlight Falls series.

Zero to 69

A sentient object shifter romance co-written with Thea Masen & Kate McDarris